Police Car
on Patrol

Peter Bently

Illustrated by Martha Lightfoot

Constable Kitt is getting Police Car ready for **night patrol.**

Sergeant Mogg receives an **alert.**

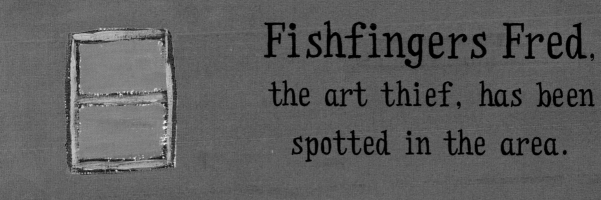

Fishfingers Fred,
the art thief, has been
spotted in the area.

The police cats are going
to the City Art Gallery to keep **watch.**

Constable Kitt gets in and puts on her seat belt.
Police Car's powerful engine **roars** into life.

On the way, Sergeant Mogg tells Constable Kitt about
Fishfingers Fred. He only steals paintings of **fish**.

There is a **famous** painting of some fish at the City Art Gallery.

Police Car soon reaches the gallery.

Constable Kitt **turns off** the lights and parks down a side street opposite the gallery.

Suddenly, they see someone climbing out of a window, carrying something large and wearing a mask.

Constable Kitt turns on Police Car's extra-bright headlights.

"Stop! Police!" booms Sergeant Mogg.

The thief **runs away** from the police cats,
quickly climbs into a getaway car...

...and **speeds** off!

NEE-NAW NEE-NAW!

Sergeant Mogg switches on Police Car's siren and flashing lights.

They **speed** around corners and **whizz** down empty streets.

The thief is fast, but Constable Kitt has had special training and can drive **quickly** and **safely**.

The pilot **radioes**
Police Car.
"I've got the thief
in my searchlight!
He's turning north."

They head north into a forest but the trees block the pilot's view. Then Constable Kitt spots a track with **fresh tyre marks!**

At the end of the track is a **dark hut.** Constable Kitt switches off Police Car's lights.

Sergeant Mogg agrees to go round the back while Constable Kitt goes in the front.

Sergeant Mogg **slips** around the side of the hut.
"Now!" he whispers into his walkie-talkie.

Constable Kitt **forces open** the front door.

The thief runs
out the back.
But Sergeant Mogg
is **waiting!**

Sergeant Mogg pulls the mask off the thief.
It's Fishfingers Fred!

"You're under arrest," Sergeant Mogg says.
He puts handcuffs on Fishfingers Fred.

The **back-up** vehicles have arrived.
Fishfingers Fred is shut inside the police van.

"**Congratulations, Officers,**"
says the Superintendent. "Now we can return
the paintings so **everyone** can enjoy them!"

"Thank you," says Sergeant Mogg.
"But we couldn't have done it without Police Car!"

Let's look at
Police Car

Speaker

Two-way radio

Powerful engine

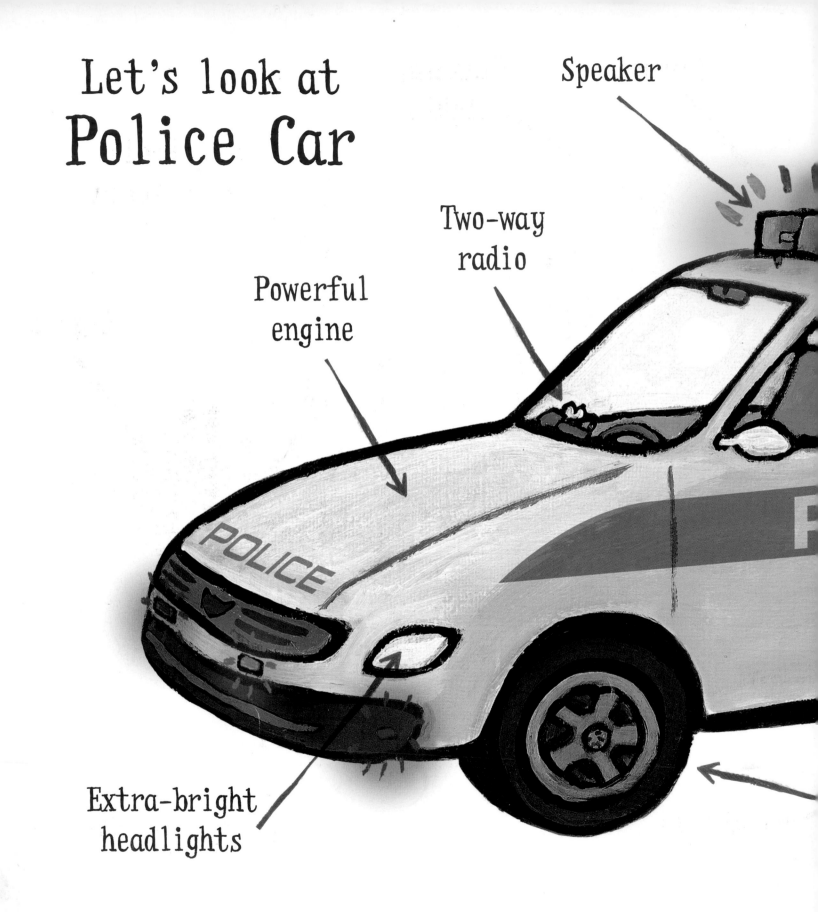

POLICE

Extra-bright headlights

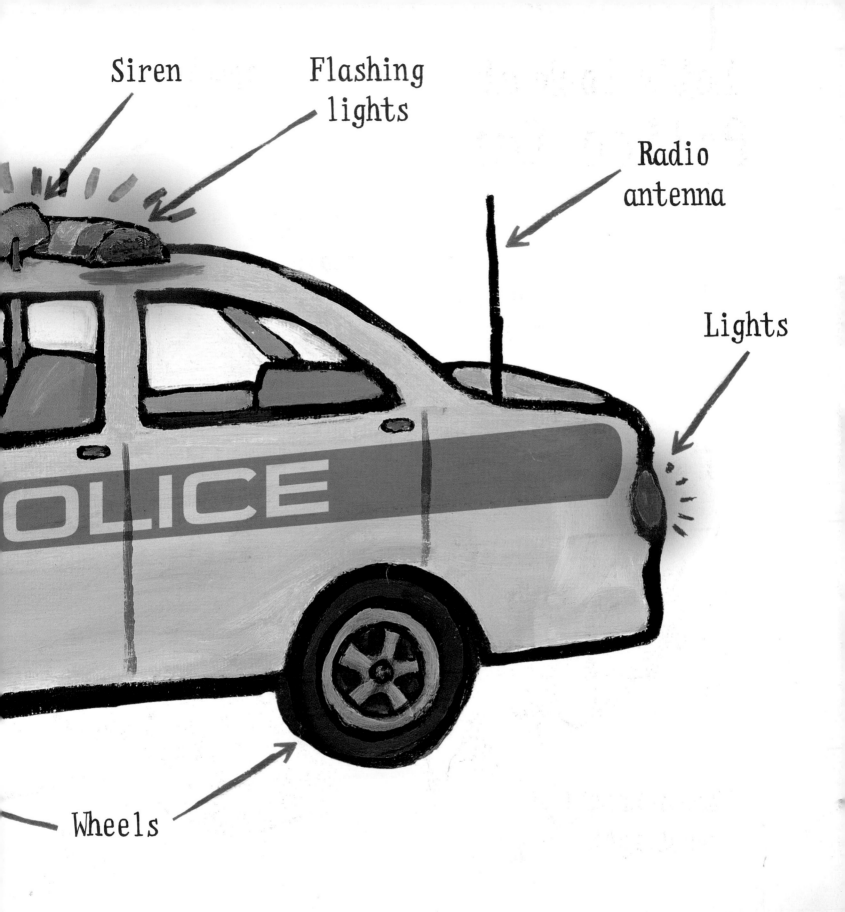

Siren

Flashing lights

Radio antenna

Lights

POLICE

Wheels

Other Police Vehicles

Police van

Police motorcycle

Police helicopter

Police bicycle

For my grandpa, who painted fish. M.L.
For Eli. P.B.

Designer: Plum5 Limited
Project Editor: Lucy Cuthew
Editorial Assistant: Tasha Percy

Copyright © QED Publishing 2013

First published in the UK in 2013 by
QED Publishing
A Quarto Group company
The Old Brewery, 6 Blundell Street
London, N7 9BH

www.qed-publishing.co.uk

A catalogue record for this book is available from the British Library.

ISBN: 978 1 78171 090 6

Printed in China